Usborne
Sticker Dollies
Baby Dragon

Zanna Davidson

Illustrated by Katie Wood
Cover illustration by Antonia Miller

Use the stickers to dress the Dolls on the 'Meet the Dolls' pages

Meet the Magic Dolls

Grace, Lily and Holly are the 'Magic Dolls'.
They care for the magical creatures, from
unicorns to fairies and mermaids, that live
on the Enchanted Isle.

Grace

is fascinated by all
magical creatures. She
reads books on how to
care for them and spends
as much time as she can
on the Enchanted Isle.

Holly

has a special relationship
with the trees and
woodland creatures in the
Spellwood. She also loves
the mermaids that live by
the Sparkling Shore.

Lily

has a passion for
flowers and fairies. She is
brilliant at healing magical
creatures with her herbs
and flower potions.

Dolly Town

The Magic Dolls live in Honeysuckle Cottage, in Dolly Town, home to all the Dolls. The Dolls work in teams to help those in trouble and are the very best at what they do, whether that's fashion design, ice skating or puppy training. Each day brings with it an exciting new adventure…

The **Shooting Star** train whisks the Dolls away on their missions.

Madame Coco's **Costume Emporium** has everything the Dolls might need.

The Dolls love to celebrate at the **Cupcake Café.**

Rose Theatre

Animal Sanctuary

Bluebell Bookshop

Evergreen Sports Arena

Royal Palace

Heartbeat Dance Academy

Palm Tree Film Studios

Fashion Design Studio

Mission Control Centre lets the Dolls know who's in trouble and where to go.

Pop Star Stadium

Silver Sparkles Skating Rink

Strawberry Lane Stables

Honeysuckle Cottage is home to the Magic Dolls.

Chapter One

Off to Dragon Rock

It was a bright, sunny day in Dolly Town and the Magic Dolls were sitting in their garden.

"I can't stop thinking about our last mission to the Enchanted Isle," said Holly, as they headed back to their cottage. "It was so amazing to meet the mermaids."

"And it was so kind of the Mer Queen to give us our necklaces," added Grace. "Now we can call on the mermaids if we ever need them."

"I wonder what our next mission will be…" said Lily. "Will it be to help the unicorns again? Or the fairies?"

"We're about to find out," said Holly. "Look!" All of their watches had started flashing.

Holly quickly picked up her screen.

"Mission Control here," said a voice. "We need all three Magic Dolls."

"We're all here," Holly replied, as Grace and Lily gathered round.

What's happened?

There's a
baby dragon
in TROUBLE
on the Enchanted Isle.
He's only recently hatched and his
parents are nowhere to be seen.

"Poor little thing," exclaimed
Grace. "I hope his parents are okay."
"There are other baby dragons
hatching over in the Far Mountains,"

Mission Control went on, "so all the dragons are busy caring for their young ones. It's that time of year when all magical creatures have their babies, and the fairies are rushed off their feet. Do you think you could look after the baby dragon until his parents return?"

"We'd love to," said Grace.

"Sending through the mission details now."

MISSION LOCATION:

The Enchanted Isle

Fairy Palace

Fairy Ring

Silver Stream

Spellwood

Pixie Meadows

MISSION INFORMATION:

The Baby Dragon

← 40 cm long →

Twinkly
dark eyes

30 cm
high

Shiny green
body

Male
Species: Unknown

"We'll be there as soon as we can," said Grace. "I'll take our book on magical creatures," she added. "It might help us."

"And I'll take my telescope and map of the Enchanted Isle," added Holly.

As soon as everyone was ready, the Magic Dolls hurried out of the door. "First stop, Madame Coco's Costume Emporium!" said Lily. "A dragon mission – I can't wait!"

The Magic Dolls ran across Dolly Town and it wasn't long before they were standing in front of Madame Coco's Costume Emporium.

"I always love coming here," said Lily, as they crossed the entrance hall to the famous glass elevator.

Floor 9
Theatre costumes

Floor 8
Dance Outfits &
Accessories

Floor 7
Magical Dept. Floor

Floor 6
Royal Dept. Floor

Floor 5
Ballet Costumes &
Accessories

Floor 4
Pop Star &
Movie Star Outfits

Floor 3
Animal Rescue
Outfits & Equipment

Floor 2
Sports Clothes &
Equipment

Floor 1
Horse Riding
& Accessories

Ground Floor
Weddings &

"Good morning, Jasper," said Grace, smiling at the lift attendant. "Can you take us to the Magical Department floor, please?"

Of course!

As soon as they were all inside, Jasper pressed the button and the lift WHOOSHED up and up, coming to a stop with a gentle

TING!

When the lift doors opened,

there was Madame Coco, smiling in welcome.

"Hello, Magic Dolls," she said. "How can I help you today?"

"We're off to the Enchanted Isle to care for a baby dragon," said Holly. "We need mission clothes, please, and anything that will help us to look after the dragon."

"Ah!" said Madame Coco. "Dragons! They're such wonderful creatures! I'll dress each of you in colours to match the elements – air and fire and water – as dragons are

drawn to them. That may help
keep the baby dragon calm."

She turned to her assistants, calling out a list of items to find for the baby dragon. Then she began to glide around the room, picking out outfits for each of the Dolls.

"Holly," she said, "I'm going to dress you as 'water' in flowing blues and greens. Grace, you will be 'fire' in a flame-red outfit. And Lily, I think you should be 'air'. I know just the dress. Its material is like wisps of cloud."

Holly's clothes

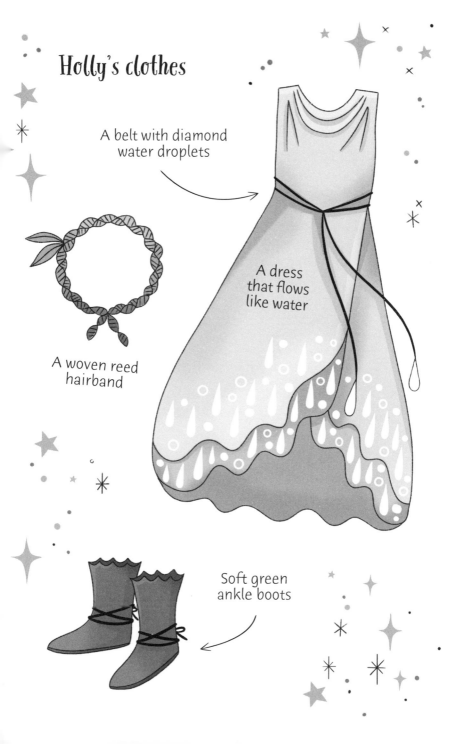

A belt with diamond water droplets

A woven reed hairband

A dress that flows like water

Soft green ankle boots

Grace's clothes

A tunic the colour of flames

A headband with flame decoration

Red and gold cropped trousers

Flame-edged ankle boots

Lily's clothes

A skirt and top as wispy as a cloud

A flower hair garland

Fluffy ankle boots

Madame Coco handed them their clothes and the Dolls stepped into the changing rooms…

When they stepped out again,
they were dressed and ready for
their mission.

"Just one more thing…" said Madame Coco, handing each of them a cloak. "You never know what the weather will be like on the Enchanted Isle."

Then she rang her little silver bell and her assistant hurried over.

"These are for the baby dragon," Madame Coco went on.

A bottle to feed him with

A blanket to keep him warm

A bowl for his food

"Thank you," said Holly, "for everything. We'd better be going. We want to get to the baby dragon as soon as we can."

The Dolls hurried over to the elevator and waved goodbye.

"Good luck!" Madame Coco called after them.

Back on the street,
Lily tapped the star symbol on
her watch. "Time to catch the
Shooting Star train," she
announced.

A moment later, a sleek train
drew up beside them in a cloud
of glittering dust.

31

"To Dragon Rock on the
Enchanted Isle, please," said Lily.
"Climb aboard!" said Sienna.
The Shooting Star train sped
through Dolly Town, then down a
dark tunnel, sparkling with stars.

With a
WHOOSH
the train shot out the other side...

There lay the Enchanted Isle. Its clear blue waters sparkled in the sun and the trees waved their branches in the breeze.

"I can't travel across the Enchanted Isle in case I disturb the magical creatures," Sienna explained, as the train glided to a halt, "but it's only a short walk from here to Dragon Rock."

"Thank you, Sienna," said Holly. "Dragon Rock, here we come!"

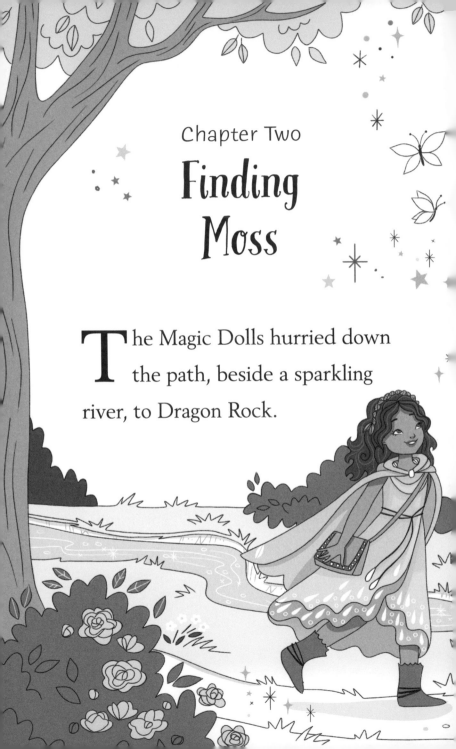

Chapter Two

Finding Moss

The Magic Dolls hurried down the path, beside a sparkling river, to Dragon Rock.

"Gosh!" said Lily. "I always forget how beautiful it is here. But it's so windy! I'm glad we've got our cloaks."

"Me too," said Grace, wrapping herself in her cloak's flame-red folds.

They hadn't gone far when the trees parted and there stood Dragon Rock, its lofty heights hidden in wisps of cloud.

Lily studied the Mission Map.

"It looks like the baby dragon is on the north face of the rock," she said. "So we'll need to walk round to find him."

"I wonder what's happened to his parents?" said Grace, as they circled the rock. "I do hope they come back soon."

"We'll just have to care for him as best we can until they return," said Lily.

They looked up from their conversation to see Holly a little way ahead, gazing up at the cliff face through her telescope.

"Hmm," she said. "I think this mission is going to be tricky." She pointed towards a jutting ridge, just beneath the peak. "Look up there," she said, passing Grace her telescope. "At that little green dot. I think that's our dragon."

"Oh no!" said Grace. "I don't think Mission Control realised how high he was going to be."

"We can't climb," said Holly. "There are hardly any footholds and it would be dangerous climbing back down, trying to hold him at the same time."

"I've read about baby dragons," said Grace, "and I know they can fly from birth. We'll just have to get the dragon to come to us."

"Good idea," said Holly. "We'll need to attract his attention first."

She cupped her hands around her mouth to make her voice louder. "Little Dragon!" she called.

Grace waved her arms in the air and Holly called again.

Coo-eee!
Li-ttle Dra-gon!

"Oh! He's looking at us!" said Lily, peering through the telescope. "He's moved closer to the edge."

This time, Grace and Holly called together. The baby dragon flapped his little wings…but nothing happened.

"Hmm," said Lily. "Maybe there's a special call we need to make?"

"Yes! That's it!" cried Holly. "We need to call to the dragon like his mother would."

Grace pulled out their book on magical creatures and began leafing through. "Here we go," she said.

Mother dragons call to their babies with a special sound. It starts as a low rumble and then becomes high pitched at the end.

Each call lasts for around ten seconds.

It sounds something like this:

Grrraaa-eeeeek!

Lily cupped her hands to her
mouth.

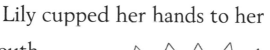

Grrraaaaaaaa
-eeeeeeek!

Again, nothing
happened.
"Maybe you didn't
go up enough at
the end?"
wondered Grace.
She handed
Lily the book,
then climbed the

little hill behind them, and called
out to him. This time, without a
moment's doubt, the dragon
flapped his little wings and took off
from the cliff edge towards them.

"Oh! Isn't he sweet!" gasped Lily.

The baby dragon was a clumsy
flier, veering this way and that,
his wings flapping furiously.

Grace held out her arms and he flew straight into them. Instinctively, she hugged him to her and smiled as his little head rested on her shoulder.

Holly wrapped the blanket around him to keep him warm. "He's gorgeous," she said, gently stroking him. "His eyes are like the night sky. What are we going to call him?"

"How about Moss?" said Grace. "To suit his shining green scales!"

"Perfect," said Lily. "Now we just need to work out what kind of dragon he is, so we know what to feed him." She opened up the book.

TYPES OF DRAGON - A FIELD GUIDE

It's extremely difficult to tell most baby dragons apart. For many species, it is impossible to tell what they are until they are at least one year old.

One year old dragons - changes just beginning to show

Small, rounded bumps on back and tail

COMMON GREEN DRAGON

Pointed wings
and spikes

EMERALD
FIRE-DRAGON

Breathes
out glitter

GLITTER
DRAGON
(very rare)

"He could be an Emerald-Fire Dragon?" said Grace, doubtfully.

"Or a Common Green?" suggested Lily.

"Or a Flaming Inferno?" said Holly, turning the page.

They all looked him over.

"No," said Grace, "it's impossible to tell."

"Well," said Lily, "it says here that most baby dragons like to eat snarkle berries, prickle fruit and crinkle leaves, so let's start with those."

"Grace, do you want to stay here and cuddle the dragon," said Holly, "if I go and look for the food?"

"And I'll go down to the river and fill his bottle with water," said Lily. "He's sure to be thirsty."

But when Holly came back
with food, the baby dragon refused
everything they offered him. The
only thing he would take was
water from the bottle.

"This isn't good," said Grace,
looking worried. "He has to eat
soon. Maybe he's unwell?"

Suddenly the dragon gave a
little cough.

"Stand back everyone!" said
Grace, expecting to see a spurt
of flame. But instead, out came
a spray of rainbow glitter. "Wow!"
she gasped.

He must be a
Glitter Dragon!

"They're really rare. No wonder he didn't want any of the food we were offering."

"What do Glitter Dragons eat?" asked Holly.

"I know it's something special," said Lily, turning to the chapter on Glitter Dragons. "Here we are.

 They eat sparkle berries, and they only grow...on the clifftops of Shimmer Island!"

"Shimmer Island?" said
Holly, checking her map. "Oh
dear – how are we ever going
to get there?"

Chapter Three

Stormy Seas

Grace and Holly gazed away from Dragon Rock and out across the sea. They could just

make out Shimmer Island,
sparkling on the horizon.

"It's too far for us to swim,"
said Holly, looking through her
telescope again. "I know!" she
exclaimed. "We could build a raft
and ask the mermaids to help
push us across."

"Brilliant!" said Lily.

At once, Lily and Holly set about collecting fallen vines and branches, before dragging them down to the edge of the river. There, Grace tied the branches together with vines,

while Moss looked on with interest.
Every now and then he made little
mewing noises.

"Don't worry, Moss," said Grace,
trying to soothe him. "We'll find
you some food as soon as we can."

Once Grace had tied the last of the branches, they all looked down at their work. "The raft looks stable," she said. "Let's see if it floats."

Together, they pushed the raft into the river, with Grace holding onto a twisted rope of vine she'd attached to the edge.

"Well it's floating!" said Holly. "So that's a good start!"

"And I've found the perfect branch for an oar," added Lily. "Let's ride the raft downriver to the sea.

Then when we get there, we can call the mermaids to come and help."

Holly climbed on board and the others followed, with Moss in Grace's arms.

"Moss doesn't seem too afraid," said Holly, smiling. "It's as if he trusts you completely, Grace."

"I know," said Grace, stroking his smooth back. "I just hope we don't let him down."

Lily steered the raft downstream, avoiding the low-hanging branches. As the river met the sea, Holly reached for her shell necklace.

"Time to call the mermaids," she said, her voice sounding a little nervous. "I hope this works."

She blew
gently over
the tiny shells
on her necklace,
just as the Mer
Queen had said.

For a moment, nothing
happened. Lily tried to paddle as
fast as she could, but it was slow
going against the tide. "It'll take us
hours to reach Shimmer Island
without the mermaids," she said.
"I do hope they come."

They all looked anxiously at
Moss, who was growing quieter
by the minute. He was still
making his little mewing noises,
but they were fainter than before,
and he seemed to lie very still in
Grace's arms.

"Maybe all the mermaids are busy?" said Grace, her voice filled with worry.

But then came a gentle humming sound, followed by a song that sounded as if it was made from foam and wind and sky.

"The mermaids!" cried Holly. "I hear them!"

They glanced down to see dark
shapes under the waves.

Then the water parted and up
rose their friend, Nerissa, followed
by three other mermaids.

"You called us!" said Nerissa,
smiling at the Magic Dolls.

"Thank you so much," said Holly.
"We need to reach Shimmer Island
as fast as we can. This baby dragon
only eats the sparkle berries that
grow there. Could you help us by
pushing the raft?"

"Of course," said Nerissa. "But it's set to be a stormy day. Do you have to go now?"

"I'm afraid so," Grace said. "I don't know how much longer this little dragon can last without food."

"Then hold on tight," said Nerissa. "The weather's coming in fast!"

The Dolls followed Nerissa's gaze,

to see large dark clouds gathering to the east, where the waves seemed to rise higher even as they watched them.

The mermaids began to push the raft through the water. Lily tried to paddle, to help speed them along, but soon the waves were too rough for her to keep her balance.

"Just focus on keeping your grip," said Nerissa, her voice calm as she powered them through the water.

By now the storm clouds were gathered directly above them and the waters were rising and falling so the raft lurched up and down.

The Dolls wrapped their cloaks tightly around themselves, and Grace clung to Moss, shielding him from the splashing waves.

The Magic Dolls held tighter still as the raft passed through a narrow gap, jagged rocks rising up

on either side, and then, at last, they touched down on the sandy shore of Shimmer Island.

"Thank you so much for bringing us here," said Holly.

As the Dolls leaped from the raft, dragging it up the beach, the mermaids watched from the water, to make sure they were safely ashore.

"Just call when you need us to

bring you back," said Nerissa.
Then, with a final wave, they
all dived back beneath the
foaming waves.

"I hope these sparkle berries are easy to find," said Grace, as they began to climb. "Moss's getting weaker and weaker. We have to find him some food…and fast!"

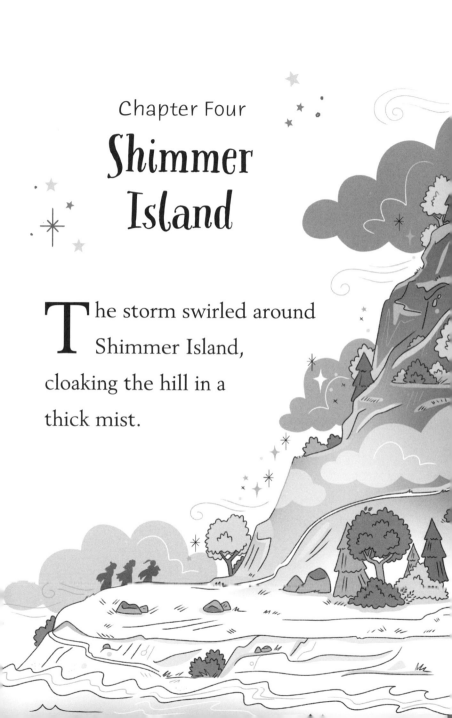

Chapter Four

Shimmer Island

The storm swirled around Shimmer Island, cloaking the hill in a thick mist.

"According to the book, the sparkle berries grow right at the very top," said Lily. "It's going to be a tricky climb in this mist."

"How *are* we going to find the berries?" asked Grace. "I can't even see beyond my hands!"

"Up ahead!" cried Lily suddenly. "Sparkling through the mist! Those *must* be the berries."

"Yes!" said Lily, with a sigh of relief. "That's them! They match the picture in the book."

At once, the Magic Dolls
set about picking them.

Then Lily chose a few of the
juiciest, plumpest berries and
scattered them into Moss's bowl.

Moss sniffed them first, then
with a happy grunting noise,
he began munching
the berries as fast
as he could.

"He looks better already," said Grace, contentedly.

His skin is brighter and look how his ears have perked up.

When Moss had eaten enough,
he flapped his wings and flew in
circles above their heads, leaving a
glittering rainbow trail in the sky.

"Well done, Moss!" laughed
Grace. "But I don't want you to get
tired." And she called out to him
again, "Grrraaaaaaaa-eeeeeeek!"
Instantly, the little dragon
returned to Grace, snuggling down
so he was cradled
in her arms.

Grace rocked him gently until he began to make little snoring noises. "He's gone to sleep," she whispered. "He must feel happy now he's got a full tummy."

"It's not long till nightfall," said Holly. "Do you think we're going to have to spend the night here?"

"It certainly looks that way," said Lily. The light was fading fast and already she could see the first stars shining through the mist.

"Oh my goodness!" said Holly, suddenly. "Look over there – coming through the cloud!"

And there, shining green and trailing clouds of glitter, came two of the biggest dragons they had ever seen.

"I think the darker one must be Moss's father," said Grace. "He's

come back for him at last!"

"Maybe the paler one is
Moss's mother?" suggested Holly.
"Female dragons can grow even
larger than the males. Either
way, they're coming towards us…
and fast."

They could see the dragons
more clearly as they flew closer.

"Um… Has anyone else noticed that the dragons don't seem very happy?" said Lily.

"Uh oh!" said Grace. "Maybe they think we've stolen their baby? I hope they're not going to attack!"

Chapter Five

Dragon Rides

T he Glitter Dragons came closer and closer on their wide, beating wings.

"What do we do?" said Lily. "How do we let them know we were only helping?"

Grace glanced down at Moss, who was stirring in her arms.

"Wake up, little dragon. I think we might need your help."

She turned to the others. "If the dragons see that Moss is safe, hopefully they'll understand."

Moss blinked open his bright, black eyes. Grace turned him, so he could see the other dragons, flying towards them.

At once, Moss began flapping
his wings in excitement. He
launched himself in the air
and flew towards them,
squeaking excitedly.

The father dragon hovered in the air, gently touching noses with Moss. Then he scooped him up in his giant claws and landed on the edge of the island, tucking him beneath his chin. The air hummed with his deep, rumbling, purring noises. The other Glitter Dragon landed beside him, and looked down at Moss, snuggled between them. Her eyes shone with pride.

"They're definitely a family," said Lily, watching them with a smile.

"Look!" said Holly. "The father has scratches down his side."

"Maybe the father dragon was in trouble and the mother had to leave to help him?" wondered Lily.

"They obviously care deeply about their baby," added Grace. "If only we could speak dragon."

By now, Moss was making more squeaking noises, and looking over at the Magic Dolls.

"I think he's telling them about us," said Holly.

Once Moss had quietened, the mother and father dragon approached them, their great heads bent as if in thanks.

"We did our best to care for him," said Grace, hoping the dragons would understand the tone of her voice, if not the words. Bravely, she reached out her hand, and touched the tip of the father dragon's nose. She smiled and was sure the father dragon smiled in return.

Then the father dragon
stretched out his wings and Moss
jumped onto his back.

"Oh!" said Grace. "They must
be going back to their nest on
Dragon Rock."

But the mother dragon had stretched out her wings too, and was nodding at them, as if to invite the Magic Dolls onto her back.

Grace turned to the others. "Do you think they're offering to fly us back to Dragon Rock?"

I've never flown on a dragon before!

Holly stepped forward, reaching out to touch the mother dragon's nose. "I don't think we have a choice," she said. "We'll never get back across the sea in this storm." She took a deep breath. "Here goes!"

Holly walked slowly over to the mother dragon and climbed the shimmering scales on her back, until she was sitting astride her. She was warm to the touch, like baked earth at the end of a sunny day.

"You're brave, Holly!" said Lily. "Well, if you can do it, so can I!"

And she joined her on the dragon's
back, wrapping her arms around
Holly's waist.

"What about you, Grace?"
asked Lily.

Grace looked at Moss, who leaped up in the air, fluttering his wings excitedly. "I'll ride with Moss!" she said, smiling.

She climbed onto the father dragon's back, gripping on tightly with her legs, while Moss snuggled into her arms.

The father dragon glanced behind, as if to check his passengers were safe, then he took to the sky.

Grace felt a strange lurching feeling in her tummy as they left the ground far below.

For a moment, all
she could do was cling on
tightly and close her eyes.

But then she became used to
the smooth, beating rhythm of
the dragon's wings. When she
opened her eyes again, they were
above the clouds. Holly and Lily
were flying beside her, their faces
lit up with wonder.

Isn't this amazing! It feels like a dream.

Everything was calm and peaceful. There was inky blackness all around, but for the stars, shining bright and clear in the darkness.

In Grace's arms, Moss seemed
utterly at home, as if he belonged
among the stars. The dragons
swooped on, and Grace looked
behind them, to see a glittering
rainbow, spreading across the sky.

"I wish this flight could last
forever," Grace whispered to Moss.

Soon the dragons began to drop down, through the clouds, until the Enchanted Isle came into view. Grace could make out the Silver Stream, winding its way across the island, and the peak of Dragon Rock, ringed by cloud.

With a final swoop, the dragons landed gently by the foot of Dragon Rock.

"Thank you," said Grace, leaning forward to hug the father dragon. "That was magical."

Chapter Six

The Cupcake Café

"Our work here is done," said Grace, a tinge of sadness in her voice.

Each of the Magic Dolls said goodbye to the dragons, then Grace gave Moss one last hug.

"We'll come back and see you again soon," said Lily. "It's going to be fun watching you grow!"

Then Moss
flapped his wings
until he was hovering in the
air above them, and blew a
cloud of glitter over Grace.

Holly and Lily laughed. "I think those are Glitter Dragon kisses," said Holly.

"And here are Magic Doll kisses," said Grace, kissing Moss on the nose.

Moss blushed bright red in response, then shot up into the air, landing on his father's head.

Then they all waved
as the dragons took to
the sky, flying to the
peak of Dragon Rock.

As the Magic Dolls turned to go, they heard a splashing sound, and a voice calling to them from the river. There was Nerissa, swimming towards them.

"I came to say goodbye," said Nerissa.

I saw the dragons land on Shimmer Island, and hoped they'd fly you back.

"They did," said Holly. "It was our first flight by dragon!"

"And much better than by stormy sea," laughed Nerissa. "Goodbye," she said, slipping beneath the surface.

"Goodbye," Holly called, "and thank you."

The Magic Dolls walked back to
where their journey had begun. Holly
tapped the star symbol on her watch
and a moment later, the Shooting
Star appeared in a swirl of stars.

"Hello, Magic Dolls," said Sienna.

"Another successful mission?"

"We've sailed through a storm, climbed a cliff and flown on the backs of dragons. It's time for a cup of hot chocolate! To the Cupcake Café, please."

Back in Dolly Town, the train drew up beside the Cupcake Café.

"Enjoy your hot chocolates," said Sienna.

"Would you like to join us?" asked Lily.

Sienna smiled but shook her head. "I've just had a call from the Princess Dolls," she said. "I need to take them to the high mountains to help a princess in trouble."

The Dolls hurried inside the café, taking their favourite seats in the cosy corner at the back.

"Sounds like it's a busy day in Dolly Town for missions," said Maya, the café owner. "Hot chocolates for you all?"

"Yes please," said Holly. "With marshmallows and cream on top!"

"I can't wait to go back to the Enchanted Isle," said Grace.

"Me too," said Lily.

"Me three!" laughed Holly.

She put out her hand, and the others followed. Grinning, they placed their hands, one on top of the other.

Magic Dolls forever!

The End

Join the **Princess Dolls** in an exciting royal adventure

Read on for a sneak peek...

It was a cold day, and the Princess Dolls were gathered in the palace drawing room, enjoying some delicious hot tea and cake.

"Isn't the chocolate cake wonderful?" said Olivia. "I think it's Chef's best yet."

"We must let her know," said Meera, looking down at the last of the crumbs on her plate. "Sophia," she added. "You've hardly touched yours."

"Oh!" said Sophia, looking up from her book. "I've been too caught up with reading about the Majestic Isle. I'm so excited we've been invited to the Cloud

Princess's Welcome Ceremony."

"I can't wait to meet the Cloud Princess and see the Sky Castle," added Olivia.

"But first," said Sophia. "We'll need to collect our outfits. It's time to visit…"

"Madame Coco's Costume Emporium!" they all chanted together.

Edited by Lesley Sims and Stephanie King
Designed by Hannah Cobley

First published in 2020 by Usborne Publishing Ltd.,
Usborne House, 83-85 Saffron Hill, London EC1N 8RT, England.
usborne.com Copyright © 2020 Usborne Publishing Ltd. UKE